Fugue: The Cure

A Science-Fiction Thriller

by S.D. Stuart

Summary

Elizabeth had everything. She was the head researcher at the largest hospital in the largest city on the colony world, Voltaire, and was constantly rebuffing marriage proposals from the wealthiest men in town.

In one instant, everything changed.

Caught between her bright future as a research scientist for the Empire, and the stigma of her past as the daughter of an outspoken protestor against the Empire, Elizabeth is forced to help a known terrorist escape from Voltaire, putting her life and her future in jeopardy.

Fugue: The Cure is a short science-fiction novel from the inventive mind of Steve DeWinter (writing as S.D. Stuart), bringing his action-packed storytelling format to the short-story science-fiction genre.

This book is a work of fiction. References to real people, events, establishments, organization, or locales are intended only to provide a sense of authenticity, and are used fictitiously. All other characters, and all incidents and dialogue, are drawn from the author's imagination and are not to be construed as real.

Ramblin' Prose Publishing

Copyright © 2013 Steve DeWinter

www.stevedw.com

eBook Edition
ISBN-10: 1-61978-008-9
ISBN-13: 978-1-61978-008-8

Trade Paperback Edition
ISBN-10: 1-61978-009-7
ISBN-13: 978-1-61978-009-5

Author's Note

I am a long form author. By that, I mean, I love to write full-length novels and actually find it hard to hold myself back when writing an 8,000 word story.

But when the writing assignment called for a short story as part of a larger anthology, I forced myself to keep the story small, with as few characters as possible, in the hope that it wouldn't explode into a larger story.

This "short story" begs for more and someday I would love to return to this world, either by expanding this story out to a full-length novel, or writing other stories. Either way, this book barely scratched the surface of the potential for the Fugue universe.

But then again, it is for the readers to decide if they want more. We shall see, after I release this short book to the wild, if there is a demand for more stories set in the Fugue universe.

Thank You

Even short books like this one require the same level of attention and care as full-length novels. So, for this book, I have the usual suspects to thank:

Bob Young, the first one to read this story and help me iron out some of the nagging issues.

Amy Roberts who, as always, makes me a better writer, whether I like it or not. I have learned more about being a good writer while discussing the editing comments she leaves all throughout my books.

And I can't thank my family enough for supporting me, in more ways than I can count, while I make a go at this writing thing. Dee and Josh, I love you both.

Chapter 1

As soon as the doors slid open, Simon stepped out of the monorail car and into the shoulder-to-shoulder crowd of daily commuters on the platform. He ducked his head and pushed his way forward to keep the crowd from sweeping him back into the monorail car.

He glanced over the milling throngs toward the main exit and spotted two constables searching the crowd.

A whistle shrilled to his right. He looked over to see another constable at the side exit pointing at him and yelling.

He ducked and surged through the crowd toward the constable who just blew the whistle. He stood a better chance of getting past one constable instead of two.

He fought his way through the crowd in a half crouch as he angled to the left and overshot the exit by a few feet. He peeked through the moving bodies to see if the constable had tracked his movements.

He smiled to himself as he stared at the back of the constable's head. If this was the best security the capital city of Voltaire could offer, his mission would be easier than he had expected.

He stepped out of the crowd and quickly approached the constable from behind. He was about to slip past him and out the exit when the constable spun around and jabbed an electric prod into his chest.

Arcs of electrical current sparked all around his body. If it were not for the steel mesh installed in the lining of his clothing, he would have fallen unconscious at the feet of the constable.

He yanked the prod out of the surprised constable's hands and brought it down on his head with a loud crack.

A woman screamed and the crowd surged away from the exit in a panic; leaving him standing over the body of an unconscious constable with an enforcement prod in his hand.

The two other constables on the monorail platform locked eyes with him and yelled for him to stop.

He did exactly the opposite. He dropped the electric prod and bolted through the exit, only to collide with another constable coming into the monorail station.

Simon tackled him to the ground and twisted his arm until he heard the shoulder pop out of alignment and the constable roar in pain. He was back on his feet and running down the street in a matter of seconds.

He already had a very small window of opportunity to pass his package to the people waiting for it, but that window shrank the longer the local constabulary actively pursued him. He had to find a way to get them off his tail.

And he had to do it quickly.

The searing hot ball of lead pierced his skin at the exact moment he heard the echo of the pistol. The impact of the bullet spun him off-balance and he tried his best to keep his feet under him as he ran. But his body was already going into shock and his legs failed him. He hit the slick cobblestone pavement and slid several feet to a stop.

Lying face down in the mud that seeped up between the cobblestones, he rolled his head to the side and looked up the street. Several constables approached slowly, pointing their pistols at him as he lay still on the ground.

Helpless.

No. Not helpless.

His original mission was but a distant memory, but he could still make a difference.

The bullet in his shoulder burned fiercely as he fumbled the package out of his pocket and extracted the syringe from the small copper box. He ignored the commands from the constables to drop whatever he had in his hands as he plunged the needle deep into a vein. He smiled up at them as he squeezed down on the plunger with his thumb.

The constables rushed him and swatted the needle out of his arm, but not before he injected the contents into his bloodstream.

He fought back as they wrestled him on to his stomach and handcuffed his hands behind his back.

As they roughly lifted him off the ground by his arms, he felt his nose start to run.

One of the constables flinched and turned away. "Someone get me a towel. I don't want this miscreant's bloody nose to spoil my uniform."

Chapter 2

Elizabeth checked both ways before dashing out into the street. She dodged two steam-powered carriages, and the same horse-drawn cart they both darted around, before she made it to the other side. Being a pedestrian in a large city was not one of the safest things to be, she thought. At least it kept people like her in steady demand.

She closed her umbrella and shook the rain off it as she stepped through the threshold of the Crested Wren, a fancy restaurant that took its name from some small bird that lived on the original world humans departed long before colonizing the planet where she was born.

Just inside the door, the maître d' looked up from his podium. His face lit up in a well-practiced smile. "Good evening Dr. Cureaux."

She shed her wet overcoat and placed it in the outstretched hand of the maître d'. "Is my companion here yet?"

"He has only just arrived Madame."

She smiled at the maître d'. "One day Reginald, someone's going to catch you in a lie."

The maître d' bowed slightly. "Maybe someday, Madame, but not today."

She looked across the full restaurant at her usual table and saw her companion handing an empty bread bowl to the waiter.

He glanced toward the entrance and immediately smiled when their eyes met.

As she approached the table, he stood up and pulled her chair out for her. "I was beginning to think you were never going to make it."

She settled into her chair. "Honestly, I did not think I was going to make it either. And I have you to blame."

He cocked an eyebrow. "Me?"

"As the Chief Constable over the Arouet Provinces, anything your men do is ultimately your responsibility. So, when your constables drag a wounded criminal into my hospital, it is all hands on deck."

"I thought you moved to the research department and no longer work on patients?"

"I did, and I don't. But as a senior staff member, and with scores of constables running around the halls, I was called on to make some executive decisions. You should be pleased to hear I gave your patient his own floor."

"I hope you did not do that on my account?"

She gave him a wink. "I did not do it because I am the Chief Constable's girlfriend. I did it because I could not have that many armed constables standing around spooking my other patients."

"Tell you what. After dinner, instead of going home and getting my daily recommended hours of sleep, I will go to the office and see about getting that number reduced to a reasonable level."

"Thank you. Whoever said dating the Chief Constable was a bad idea?"

"Yeah. Who would go and say an idiotic thing like that?"

She smiled at him. "You did."

"That's right. Now I remember. Oh, I took the liberty of eating all the bread before you arrived. I know how you don't like to be tempted by all those carbs."

She laughed, all the drama at the office melting away in the presence of a good friend. "How very thoughtful of you."

They spent the next hour alternating between silence and light conversation as they ate. One of the benefits of dating someone exclusively was the unspoken agreement that allowed you to stay quiet when the conversation naturally waned.

But leave it up to Chief Constable Severn Blaine to abhor silence as if it were an admission of wrongdoing.

"With the exception of tonight's interruption, how goes your research?"

"I think I'm close enough to identifying the markers that can help us end Scalars Disease."

"I don't want to sound like I'm minimizing your life's work, but what's the point? Nobody has died from Scalars in over a hundred and twenty years."

"The threat is still there."

"Not really. We have the annual immunization that keeps everyone in the Empire healthy."

"That is just a band-aid on a gaping wound. I want to do more than just sweep the problem under the rug. When you do that, it is still there. It is still under the rug. I want to cut it from the house."

"The Empire has had the best minds working on a cure for over a hundred years."

"Not all the best minds."

He winked at her. "Touché." He tilted his head to the side. "Is that why you have not accepted my marriage proposal?"

She lowered her head and fixed her eyes on the boiled potato stuck to the end of her fork. "I have to leave myself available for acceptance at the Royal Medical Society on Viktorion. It's nothing personal."

"They do accept married people in the Royal Societies."

"I cannot ask you to leave the position you worked so hard to obtain."

"That would be my choice."

"It is not a choice I want to force you to make."

The silence between them stretched on for a full minute until he crumpled his cloth napkin and placed it on the table. "I am sorry I brought it up, but I am not getting any younger and I want to start a family."

She folded her hands in her lap. "I'm sorry Severn. I'm not ready to settle down. I have too much…"

A constable appeared at the side of the

table and interrupted her. "I am sorry to disturb you sir."

Severn looked up at the man and let out an audible sigh. "What is it Alex?"

"You have an open call from the Head Magistrate on the wireless, sir."

Frown lines appeared on Severn's forehead. "The Head Magistrate?"

"Yes sir."

"From Viktorion? That Head Magistrate?"

"The very same sir."

He looked at Elizabeth. "Why would he be calling me?"

She shrugged her shoulders. "I think you better take that call."

He scooted back his chair and stood up. "I think I better. We will finish our discussion later, Liz."

She looked up at him expectantly. "I can't wait."

He took her hand and kissed it. "I'm going to convince you to marry me."

She smiled. "I know."

She watched him leave and turned away the offer for dessert from the waiter. He did not present her with a bill for dinner. Her senior position at the hospital, and the fact that she dined with the Chief Constable, made their meal gratis courtesy of the management at the Crested Wren.

She gathered her overcoat and umbrella from the maître d' and stepped back out into the light drizzle that made the Arouet Provinces famous as the wettest place in the entire system second only to Paxilla; as that planet had been engulfed by its oceans.

At this late hour, the streets were nearly deserted. She would have to walk a few blocks to get to the main thoroughfare in order to catch a taxi home. Severn was supposed to take her home but, when called away unexpectedly, knew better than to offer to leave a car for her. She worked her way up to a senior administrator position in the hospital on her own. She did not need help from anyone. And she had spent enough time in Arouet, while attending the local medical college, that she could find her way around the city blindfolded.

She walked a couple of blocks in the misty rain and rounded the corner. She jumped in surprise as she nearly collided with a man standing on the sidewalk.

He took a step backward. "I'm sorry. I did not mean to startle you."

She smiled at him. "That's okay. I was lost in thought and should have been paying more attention."

Just as she was about to pass him, he looked at her curiously.

"Excuse me ma'am, are you Elizabeth Cureaux?"

"Yes."

"Dr. Elizabeth Cureaux?"

"Yes. Do I know you?"

Someone grabbed her from behind as the

man placed a black bag over her head. She smelled the sweet scent of ether right before she lost consciousness.

Chapter 3

When she woke, she still had the black bag over her head. Her mouth was devoid of moisture and her throat burned as she swallowed dryly. She lifted her head and felt the rough scraping of the ropes on her bare arms as she struggled to move in the chair she found herself bound.

Someone ripped the bag off her head and she shut her eyes against the blinding light of the morning sun. The sound of boots echoed on the wooden floor, followed by the ruffle of a window shade as it was pulled down to mute the sunlight.

Her eyes adjusted to the room's dimmer light, but the pounding in her head was only made worse when she swiveled her neck to look around the small room. With the exception of the chair she was in, there was no other furniture in the bare room. The man with the boots let go of the shade pull-string, walked over to her and bent down. "How are we feeling?"

She swirled her tongue around her dry mouth. "I could use a glass of water."

Boots had obviously done this to other people before. He was already holding a glass of water in one hand. He held it to her mouth so she could drink and looked into her eyes. "Do you know who I am?"

She gulped hungrily at the water until she was satisfied. Only then did she answer him. "Your picture is posted prominently in every police station, government building, and hospital. I am supposed to alert the authorities immediately if I see you. I am guessing we are far enough away from the city proper that if I started screaming, nobody would be breaking down that door to rescue me."

"You may think you know who I am, but you only know what you have been told. You don't know the real me."

"Correct me if I'm wrong, but aren't you

Atlas Croft? Leader of the terrorist group, La Guérison?"

He bowed with a flourish of his hand.

"Well then, I am not instilled with confidence that you are a man of your word."

"My name means, 'He who dares.' It is from the texts of ancient Earth mythology. You see, Atlas led the Titans in a rebellion against Zeus and the other Greek gods, much like I am leading a rebellion against the Empire, and our leaders who act like they are gods; like they are somehow better than the rest of us.

"For his punishment, Atlas was condemned to bear the weight of the heavens upon his shoulders. And like that Atlas of long ago, so do I bear the weight of all the worlds in the colonies on my shoulders. It is my responsibility to succeed in our campaign against the oppressors, even as the Atlas of mythology failed."

"That's quite a god complex you have

there. In my book, your still public enemy number one. But kidnapping is not among your usual repertoire. So it begs the question, what do you want with me?"

He grinned. "You are going to get my associate out of the hospital."

"That criminal they brought in last night is one of yours?" She shook her head. "He is sequestered on his own floor and under heavy guard. Sorry, I can't help you. And even if I could, I wouldn't."

"I had the bright idea of appealing to your humanity, or sense of moral obligation, but time is of the essence, so I decided this would be quicker."

He held up a needle and syringe in his other hand.

She laughed. "I'm a doctor. You're going to have to find something scarier than that if you want to frighten me."

"It is not the needle you should be afraid of, it's what's inside." He stabbed the needle into her arm and her muscle twinged involuntarily. "Within six hours, you will start to feel the effects. Within 12 hours, you will become contagious. Within 24 hours it will be too late to administer the antidote, of which only I possess."

She struggled against the ropes. "Why are you doing this to me? I can't... I'm just a doctor. I can't sneak a patient out from under the noses of the constables."

"I think you will try." He stood up and inspected the spent syringe. "What I infected you with is something new. It took us months to develop an antidote. You don't have that kind of time. You do what I ask and I will give it to you."

"If I do this, how do I know I can trust you to give me the antidote?"

"Because I am not your enemy. I am the enemy of the Empire, and the Empire is the enemy of the people it subjugates. Since I am the enemy of your enemy, that makes me your friend."

He went around behind her and untied the ropes. They dropped to the floor, but she did not stand up. "Why me?"

"I need somebody who has unlimited access to the hospital, and a get out of jail free card from the Chief Constable. I know of only one person on the planet who meets those requirements."

"You are seriously overestimating my relationship with the Chief Constable."

"No. I do not think I am."

She looked up at the most wanted man in all the colonies. He looked softer, gentler, in person than the blurry pictures associated with the depiction of a madman in the newswires.

"I'm curious about something. You call your group La Guérison. Is that French for garrison?"

He smiled. "It is French, yes, but it means healing. It is not a military term."

"Healing?"

"The Empire is sick, and we are the cure."

He pulled a handkerchief from his back pocket and held it out to her. "Here, your nose is bleeding."

She pressed the handkerchief against her nose and pulled it away. The white handkerchief was stained a crimson red.

"Don't worry. The bleeding will stop in a minute. It just indicates that the infection is complete."

He pulled a TravelCard from his other pocket and held it out to her. "This is a one-way ticket on the shuttle to Arcadia. It leaves tonight at 8 PM. Make sure my friend is on it."

"And if I don't?"

"You're the doctor. What is the survival rate for unknown alien diseases around here?"

Chapter 4

Elizabeth stood across the street from the hospital. She fiddled with the TravelCard and noticed her hand was shaking. She took three deep breaths to steady her nerves and slipped the TravelCard in a pocket.

She walked across the street and into the hospital like it was any other day. As soon as she crossed through the front doors, she made a beeline for her office. If she could get the standard white doctor smock over her clothes, nobody would notice she wore the same thing as yesterday.

Linda, her assistant, spotted her from the other end of the hallway. "Liz!"

Elizabeth ducked her head and tried to make it to her office before she caught up with her, but Linda was faster.

"Liz. There is something you have to see."

Linda walked into the office right behind her and closed the door. Elizabeth went straight for her white coat and put it on.

Linda tossed the folder she was carrying onto Elizabeth's desk. "Take a look at these lab results."

Elizabeth picked up the folder and read it. While she did, Linda kept talking. "That man the constables brought in last night underwent surgery for four hours to extract the bullet from his shoulder. During that time, we administered a full transfusion because of the loss of blood from both the initial wound and the surgery."

She could not think about anything right now, other than how her own life hung in the balance unless she figured out a way to get an injured prisoner, under constant guard, out of the hospital, and onto that shuttle; before whatever that terrorist injected into her killed her. She looked up from the folder. "I have a lot of work to do, Linda. Can you show me this later?"

Linda ignored her. "As per protocol, I ran

the full gamut of tests before ordering blood from the bank."

She shut the folder. "Come back later. I'm busy right now."

Linda snatched the folder out of her hand, opened it, and shoved it in her face, pointing to a single result among the list of lab tests. "Look!"

She focused on the too close lab report. "He tested negative for something. So what?"

"Look what he tested negative for."

She read it.

Then she read it again.

She looked up at Linda. "That can't be right."

"I had enough of his blood to run a second test. It came up negative also."

"Something is wrong with the test."

Linda shook her head. "That's what I thought, so I withdrew some of my own blood and ran it through. I tested positive for Scalars, just like everybody else. Everybody but him."

A thought occurred to Elizabeth. "The transfusion…"

Linda nodded. "That's what I thought too. Everyone has traces of Scalars in their blood, even blood donors. I took a sample from him right after the surgery and then again a little over an hour ago. He had trace amounts of Scalars in his blood right after surgery."

"Where's the lab work from an hour ago?"

Linda pointed to the folder in her hands. "You're looking at it."

She stared at the report, not really seeing it. "You're telling me the patient does not have Scalars now?"

"I'm telling you his body killed off the Scalars we put in him with the blood transfusion."

"That's why they want him," Elizabeth whispered to herself.

"What?"

She remembered Linda was still in the

room with her and snapped the folder shut. "Good work Linda. Have you told anyone else about this?"

Linda shook her head. "Nobody else would believe me."

Elizabeth tapped the folder with a finger. "Good. We need a bigger sample of his blood. We need to find out how he fought off Scalars."

Linda hesitated for a moment; her face registered an internal battle taking place inside her head. Elizabeth had seen this look before. "You have something else to tell me Linda?"

"That's not the only strange thing about our patient. He has a tattoo of sheet music on his back."

"People tattoo weird things on themselves all the time."

"What he has tattooed on his back is a fugue, a style of music. My father was in the Voltaire Symphony and I went with him to his daily practices the whole time I was growing up, so I know a little bit about classical music and am very familiar with this particular fugue. But there were extra notes on it that didn't belong. I copied down the letters that correspond to those notes. It's on the second piece of paper."

Elizabeth flipped to the next page in the folder.

She looked up at Linda. "This looks like part of a chemical formula."

Linda nodded her head slightly. "The rest was unreadable because of the gunshot wound. Do you think this is what he injected himself with to kill Scalars?"

"He injected himself with something?"

"I overheard the constables talking. They say that right before they arrested him, he injected something into his arm. They figured he was some kind of drug addict getting his last fix before going to jail."

Elizabeth set the folder down on her desk. "I want to run some more tests. But I can't do it with the constables watching. Do you think you could help me move him?"

Linda shook her head. "They've increased the number of guards outside his room. I don't know if they will let us move him."

"If he somehow knows the cure, or even is the cure, he just might be the answer I have been searching for my entire life. I can be the one to rid the Empire of Scalars once and for all."

She stared into Linda's eyes as a smile broke across her face. "We can be the ones to eliminate Scalars."

"I am just your research assistant. I do not need to share in your glory. I will have plenty of time after you retire to find my own glory. But if it means not having to endure the annual immunization shot ever again, then I will do whatever it takes to help you."

Her smile faded as she realized what was needed to keep the patient out of the Empire's hands. "I can't ask you to break the law."

"Any law that would keep us from finding a cure is a law I will not follow."

Elizabeth smiled again at Linda. She had always known she had picked the right assistant to help her in her research. But now she was glad she had picked someone who had become a friend as well.

"I need to get him away from the constables."

Linda smiled back. "Tell me what you want me to do."

Chapter 5

Elizabeth walked down the hallway toward the prisoner's room. There were constables stationed every few feet along the hallway in addition to the two in front of his door.

As soon as she stopped at the door, the bigger of the two constables held up a hand. "I'm sorry ma'am. Nobody is allowed inside."

She gave the constable a hard stare. "Do you know who I am?"

"Yes ma'am. But the order comes from Chief Constable Blaine himself. No exceptions."

She cocked her head to one side. "Are you sure you want to explain to the Chief Constable how you let the prisoner die because you withheld necessary medical care?"

"I am afraid you have been misinformed ma'am. The doctor just authorized the prisoner's release. Chief Constable Blaine is downstairs securing the transfer wagon now."

She struggled to keep the look of surprise from registering on her face at learning that Severn was here. Instead, she stood straighter and tried to sound like the voice of authority.

"If someone has been misinformed, it is you. Policy dictates that I personally authorize all prisoner patient releases from this hospital. I will not authorize a release unless I am allowed to view the patient myself."

He refused to move out of the doorway. "You may discuss the matter with Chief Constable Blaine when he gets back."

"You are more than welcome to send Severn in when he gets back, but I am going in now." She used the Chief Constable's first name in an attempt to prove she was on better terms with his boss than the man who was only following orders.

She stepped forward and stared at the arm blocking her entry to the room.

He finally lowered his arm. She looked up at him with a mock smile. "Thank you."

Once inside the room she closed the door behind her. She quietly slid a chair over and wedged it under the door knob. Once she was certain that it was firmly stuck, she walked quickly over to the bed where the prisoner was asleep.

She touched him lightly on the non-bandage shoulder and his eyes popped open.

She placed a finger to her lips. "Shh. The police are coming to get you. If you do exactly as I say, I can get you out of here before that happens."

He sat up and winced from the pain in his shoulder. "Who are you?"

"I'd rather not say."

"Why do you want to help me?"

"A friend of yours gave me some motivation."

"You must mean Croft. He can be very convincing when he wants to be."

"I don't think I agree with you on his methods of persuasion. Nevertheless, I am here to get you out of the hospital. He also provided a TravelCard to get you on a shuttle and off Voltaire tonight."

"He's always been so accommodating."

She noticed a sheen of sweat on his skin. "How do you feel?"

"Not too good. But the doctor says I'll live."

He tried to stand up out of bed and collapsed back down on the mattress with a grunt.

She hooked an arm under his good shoulder and felt the heat radiating off his body. "Can you walk?"

He gave her sheepish grin. "If the alternative is prison, I can dance a jig if you need me to."

"That's okay. Walking will be just fine."

He leaned heavily on her and she struggled to remain standing as they shuffled away from the bed.

He breathed heavily from the exertion.

"What did you do with the guards?"

"I didn't do anything. There are still at least fifteen of them out in the hallway."

"Then how are you getting me out of here exactly?"

She nodded with her head toward the wall opposite the door. "The window."

"Oh. I didn't know we were on the ground floor."

"We're not."

They shuffled over to the window. She slid it open with one hand while still supporting nearly all his weight with the other. He leaned over slightly as he looked out the window and almost knocked her over when he took a sudden step away from it. "I am not going out that window."

"It's the only way."

"We must be a hundred stories up."

"What is your name?"

"Simon."

"Simon, we are only ten stories up."

"Might as well be a thousand. I am not going out that way."

She struggled to support his weight and hold him steady while he tried to backpedal away from the window. "The Chief Constable is on his way up here right now to take you to prison. Either we go out that window or you go with him."

"I'll take prison over being thrown out of a ten story window any day."

Linda's head popped up outside the window. "What's taking so long?"

He let out a yelp of surprise.

Elizabeth steadied him with all of her strength. "You have to be quiet."

There was a faint knock on the door followed by the muffled voice of a constable. "Is everything okay in there?"

She muscled him toward the window. "I'm not asking you to jump. We have an emergency evacuation gurney just outside the window. Just climb into it and you will be safely on the ground in less than a minute."

There was another knock at the door followed by a louder voice. "Excuse me, doctor?"

The doorknob turned and the door pushed against the chair, moving it only slightly. The constable outside banged on the door loudly. "Doctor? Open the door. Doctor!"

She maneuvered him next to the window. "I can, literally, close your window of opportunity and let you go with the nice men outside, or you can buck up and climb out onto that gurney. The choice is yours."

The constables took turns throwing themselves against the door repeatedly, the chair moving slightly with each impact.

Simon looked at the door that was now open a crack, and widening every time a constable hurled his body against it.

He looked at her and then out the window.

She took advantage of his indecision to grab onto him tightly, and they both went out the window together. They landed on the canvas gurney just as she heard the chair splinter into pieces and shouting constables flood the room.

As soon as they were on the gurney, Linda expertly tugged the release rope. They dropped quickly, slowing only when they were a few feet off the ground. The gurney nestled softly into the grass at the base of the building.

Elizabeth looked up and saw a constable's head retreat back through the window, followed by more shouting. She was too far way to hear, but she had a good idea of what was being said.

Linda helped her get Simon to his feet and they raced across the grass to Linda's waiting steam car. Together, they placed him in the backseat and Elizabeth jumped behind the driver's wheel. She held her hand up and stopped Linda from climbing in next to her. "Nobody knows that you helped me. You have a promising future as a scientist and I won't let you jeopardize that for me. Thank you for your help. And letting me borrow your car."

Linda smiled and closed the door. "You mean steal it."

Elizabeth smiled back. "Thank you."

She released the brake and the car shot forward.

She was out of the city and deep in the countryside in less than an hour. She had not told Linda where she was headed and nobody, not even Severn, knew her well enough to guess.

When asked about her family, she always said that both her parents were dead.

That was not entirely true.

Her mother was dead, but her father was very much alive, even though she had not spoken to him in over fifteen years.

She pulled to a stop in front of a dilapidated farmhouse and Simon sat up in the backseat. "This does not look like the shuttle station."

She shut down the steam engine. "We still have several hours before your flight and we need some place to hide where they won't find us."

He looked around. "Where are we?"

The front door to the dilapidated farmhouse opened up and an elderly man walked out of the house, down the front steps, and squinted in the direction of the steam car.

She closed her eyes and let out a long breath. "My father's house."

She stepped out of the car as the old man squinted even harder at her for a moment before his face registered surprise. "Lizzie?"

"Hey Pops."

"What are you doing here?"

"I didn't have anywhere else to go."

A smile spread across his face. "You know you've always been welcome."

Simon climbed out of the backseat of the car and her father did a double take. "Who's your friend?"

"He's not really…"

Simon took a half step forward on shaky legs and held his hand out. "My name is Simon."

She darted forward and grabbed Simon's arm before her father could shake his hand. "He's not well Pops."

She shot Simon an angry look. "You might still be contagious. I don't think you should be touching anyone."

Simon collapsed to the ground and hugged himself with his arms as he shivered uncontrollably.

She knelt down next to him and checked his pulse with one hand while laying the back of her other hand against his forehead. "Your symptoms are exactly that of Scalars Disease. But you tested negative for Scalars."

He looked up at her and tried to smile. It

came out more like a grimace from the pain he was obviously experiencing. "I'll be okay, I just need to rest."

And with that, he closed his eyes and went limp in her arms.

Despite her insistence that he not touch Simon, her father helped drag him into the house and upstairs to her old bedroom. She wrapped him in a wool blanket, placed him on her bed, and pressed a cold washcloth against his fevered head.

As soon as he stopped shivering in his sleep, she went out on the porch and sat in the rocking chair that looked out over the farm where she had grown up. Within a few minutes, her father sat down in the rocking chair next to her, lit his pipe, and rocked silently as he gazed out over the family farm.

"Where did I go wrong, Pops?"

He puffed at his pipe for a few moments before replying. "Near as I figure it, you're only just now doing something right."

She turned toward him, the fury building up inside her, because he was continuing the same conversation they had never ended fifteen years earlier. "I am not like you Pops. I follow the rules."

"Newswire said you helped a terrorist escape from custody."

She closed her eyes and let out a heavy sigh. "I didn't have a choice."

"We all have choices to make. And we have to live with the consequences of our choices."

"You weren't the only one who paid the consequences of your choice, Pops. You protested against the Empire, and your family paid for it. I paid for it. I was pulled out of school, and taken away for my friends, as a little girl. We were banished out here to the middle of nowhere. Your choices affected all of us."

He held the pipe close to his mouth. "It was a different time back then. I did what I thought was right."

"But my choices are not your choices. It took me a long time to rid myself of the stigma you placed on me as a child. I had to fight and claw my way to where I am now."

He puffed again at his pipe. "And just where are you now?"

She was about to tell him she was a senior researcher, at the largest hospital, in the largest city on the planet, when she remembered where she was sitting, and who she was talking to.

Her shoulders slumped. "Right back where I started."

He reached over and placed a hand on her knee. "For what it's worth, I'm very proud of you."

She looked over at her father and gave him a weak smile. She was exhausted, cold and starting to feel the effects of whatever that terrorist had injected into her. She wanted to sit all night long with her father on the front porch, like she used to as a child. But if she was going to put Simon on that shuttle, and get the antidote before it was too late, she had to leave soon.

He did not smile back and looked out over the farm. "I'm sorry."

She took his hand in hers. "No. I'm sorry. I was angry with you for so long…"

His eyebrows knitted as he continued to stare out into the distance. But he wasn't just staring vacantly at nothing; his eyes were tracking something.

She looked in the same direction, and saw several security vehicles speeding down the dirt road toward the farmhouse.

Her father spoke just above a whisper. "I'm sorry."

Chapter 6

Elizabeth sat handcuffed to the metal chair in the small room, with her head down on the table in front of her, and awaited her fate. Every muscle in her body trembled as her skin temperature alternated between freezing and boiling.

Time had lost all meaning in this tiny room without windows or a clock. From how she felt, she knew that she was nearing the point of no return for an antidote, if that time had not already elapsed.

The door opened and she lifted her head to see which of the several interrogators she would have to talk to again, just like she had been doing for countless unknown hours. She was about to ask them to adjust the temperature in the room again when she saw who walked in.

Chief Constable Severn Blaine closed the door behind him.

She leaned forward in the chair as far as the chains would allow. "I know what you're thinking Severn, but I had no choice. That terrorist, Croft, injected me with something. He said if I didn't deliver Simon to him, I would die. You have to find him and get me that antidote, if it's not already too late."

Severn sat in the chair opposite her and placed a folder in front of him on the table. He stared at her without any hint of emotion on his face. "How long have you been working with La Guérison?"

She barked out a nervous laugh. "What are you talking about? You know me Severn. I'm not a terrorist."

"When I first heard that it was you who helped Simon escape from custody, I refused to believe it."

"I can explain…"

He cut her off. "I came close to losing my commission as Chief Constable over this. I had to convince my superiors that you fooled me just as easily as you fooled everyone else."

Tears formed in the corners of her eyes. "No. You have to believe me."

"How long?"

She shook her head, the tears streaming down her cheeks. "Severn, I never…"

He slammed his fists on the table. "Stop lying to me!"

She clamped her mouth shut and could not believe this was happening.

Severn fiddled with the folder in front of him and laughed. "We stood in line together for the annual immunization. I held your hand while you endured the pain of the treatment. You did all that to keep your cover?"

"Severn, you're not making any sense."

"You certainly didn't do it because you had Scalars."

"What are you talking about?"

He opened the folder and slid it across the table at her. "We ran the test like you asked. To find out what you claim was injected in you. It was a nice diversion, but I wasn't going to let you fool me again. I had them take an extra vial; and look what I found."

She blinked away the tears and focused on the lab report in front of her. Her eyes were drawn immediately to the test for Scalars Disease. Next to it was a single word in all capital letters that should not be there.

He motioned to the folder in front of her, the rage building in him spilled out onto his face. "You tested negative for Scalars!"

She looked up at him and shook her head. "That's impossible."

The unemotional detachment of the interrogator took over in his eyes. "You tell me which of these scenarios is impossible. You are a terrorist working with La Guérison, and came here to distract me from my duties so you could start an underground terrorist transportation system or, as you say, you were injected with an antidote for Scalars by the system's most notorious terrorist himself, and were an unwilling participant in the attempt to extract a terrorist from my custody."

She could tell he had already made up his mind as to which he believed.

"Your father finally understands that the Empire has everyone's best interests at heart. You can thank him for intervening before you made the biggest mistake of your life."

She stared back down at the report that showed she did not have Scalars.

Something that was impossible stared her right in the face.

No, not impossible.

There was one explanation.

Croft had not injected her with a virus that would kill her. He had injected her with a virus that targeted Scalars. But it didn't just kill Scalars; it eradicated it completely, as if it had never been there in the first place. Then she remembered what Croft had said after he injected her.

She looked up at Severn. "Can you tell me

one thing?"

He frowned at her. "What?"

"How long have I been in this room?"

"I know it may feel like days, but you've only been in here for nine hours."

She spit in his face before he could react.

He wiped her spittle out of his eyes and stared hard at her. "Your father may have prevented you from making one mistake, but it seems that you want to make all new ones."

He closed the folder and picked it up as he stood. "We will get the rest of your friends, and remand you to the Empire Marshals. After a swift trial, you will all die a horrible death."

She watched him intently as he knocked on the door to be let out. As the door opened, she called out to him one more time. "Severn?"

He turned around, but said nothing.

She nodded at him as a smile spread across her face. "Your nose is bleeding."

Chapter 7

Emperor Augustus strode in to the war planning room and sat at the head of the long table. Every one of his trusted advisers was already seated around the table.

He did not apologize for getting everyone out of bed for this emergency meeting. "Tell me about the situation on Voltaire."

General Bacchus Cole cleared his throat.

"I received confirmation from one of our moles within La Guérison that this was part of their ongoing terror campaign against the Empire. We believe one of their agents injected himself with the virus and spread it to the population. Before we blacked out the planet's communication network, word spread around the system that people were getting sick with an unknown disease in increasing numbers. Our main office has denied thousands of requests for communication exceptions to Voltaire."

"Good. Continue to deny all requests. Nobody off-planet knows that everyone is recovering without any casualties?"

"No, your Majesty."

"And did I read my briefing correctly that this virus somehow eliminated Scalars from among those infected?"

"I have personally verified that information is correct, sir."

"I want a contingent of warships in orbit to keep anyone from getting off of Voltaire."

"Several are already en route."

"Excellent. As always, you anticipate me perfectly General."

The General bowed his head. "I live to serve."

"Voltaire is still a level four colony, correct?"

"Yes. They are not yet self-sufficient and still rely on imports from the other colonized worlds to survive."

"Inform the newswire immediately that we

will begin daily supply drops for the people of Voltaire while we search for a cure. In one month, inform the newswire that supply drops have been stopped because the entire population of the planet is dead from the plague."

"Yes your Majesty."

"And then I want you to bombard the planet until the entire surface has been reduced to ash."

Also by Steve DeWinter

Inherit The Throne

The Warrior's Code

The Red Cell Report (COMING SOON)

Written as S.D. Stuart

The Wizard of OZ: A Steampunk Adventure

The Scarecrow of OZ: A Steampunk Adventure

Fugue: The Cure

Be the first to know about Steve DeWinter's next book, and get your exclusive limited-time discount for each hot new release, the same day it hits shelves. In fact, receive your first exclusive anytime discounts in the "Welcome" Email.

Follow the URL below to subscribe for free today!

http://bit.ly/BookReleaseBulletin